You Made Me a Dad

Written by
Laurenne Sala
Illustrated by
Mike Malbrough

HARPER
An Imprint of HarperCollinsPublishers

You Made Me a Dad

www.harpercollinschildrens.com

ISBN 978-0-06-239694-5

The artist used watercolor and Adobe Photoshop to create the illustrations for this book.
Typography by Jeanne L. Hogle
19 20 21 22 23 SCP 10 9 8 7 6 5 4 3 2 1
❖
First Edition

To Lucía and her daddy, my heroes.
–L.S.

For Bella.
–M.M.

I loved you before I saw you.

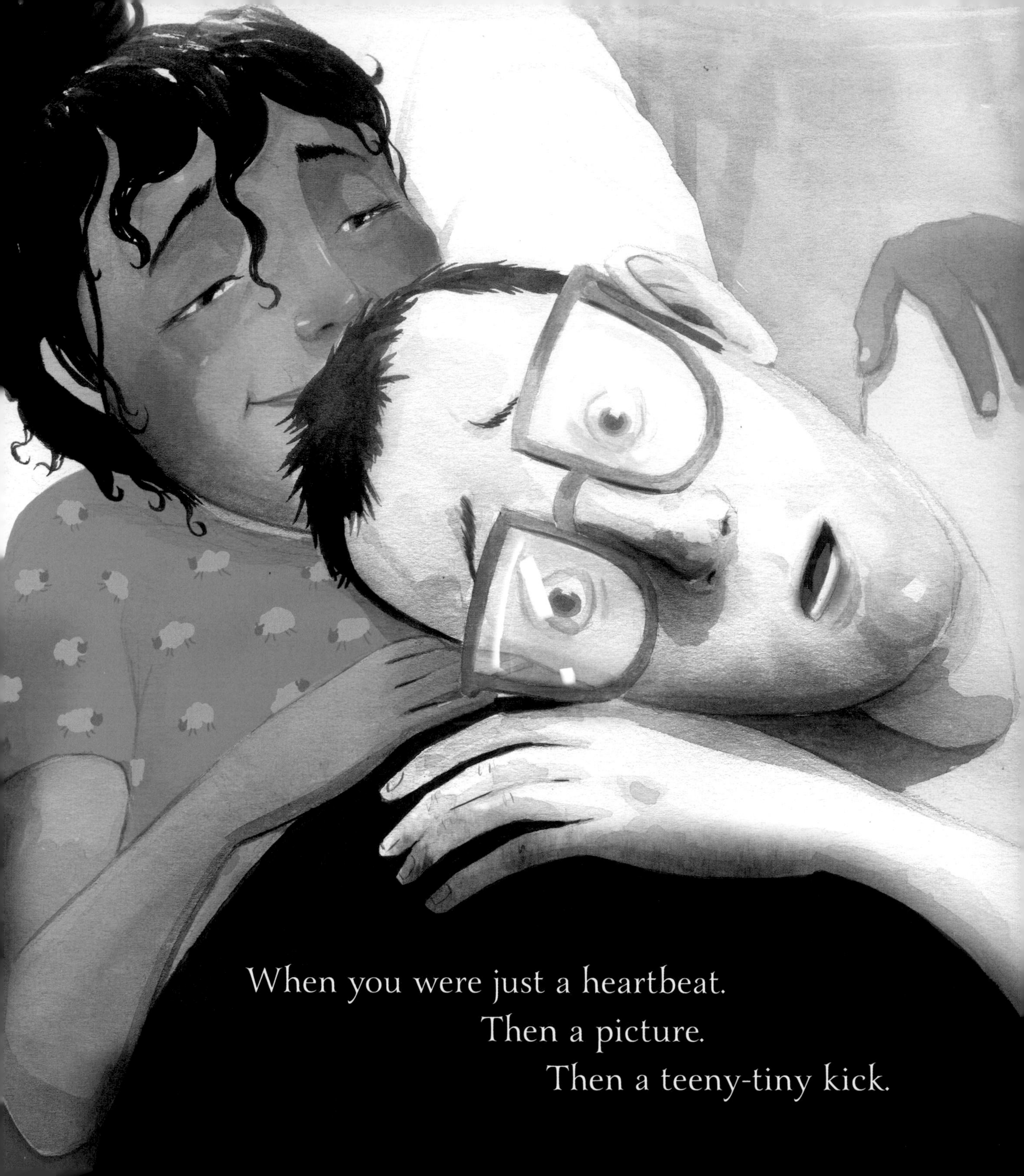

When you were just a heartbeat.
Then a picture.
Then a teeny-tiny kick.

I brought rocky road ice cream for Mommy.
And fuzzy blankets. I rubbed her feet.

I picked up all the things she couldn't see when her belly got too big.

I told her not to worry.
Then I told her not to worry . . . again.

I said different names out loud a million times.

I wondered if your eyes would look like mine.
And whose nose you would get.

But before I'd finished imagining who you'd be, you were here.

And you were perfect.

I realized right away that I had a new job. I would teach you to be kind.

To listen to good music.

To be yourself.

To make you giggle A LOT.

How lucky am I? I get to be your peekaboo partner, your horse, your tickle monster, your pillow . . .

your hero!

And you are mine.

You teach me how to draw rainbows and dinosaurs and build big forts and hide in the sneakiest spots.

Because of you, I know what monsters sound like and how to dance silly

. . . and that my heart is bigger than anything on Earth. (And in outer space, too.)

I promise to always be lovey and laughy with you.

To teach you big words even if you can't pronounce them.
To throw you up HIGH in the air but never ever drop you.

To take time to listen
to your dreams.

And your stories.

And to answer *allll* your questions.
Even the silliest ones.

Sometimes I'll make mistakes. I might lose your socks. Or forget the instructions.

But we'll giggle about it. And make it fun. You always make life more fun.

One day, I will put your little feet on top of my gigantic feet,

and we will walk around the whole world together.

And somewhere, in the middle, I will tell you a story.

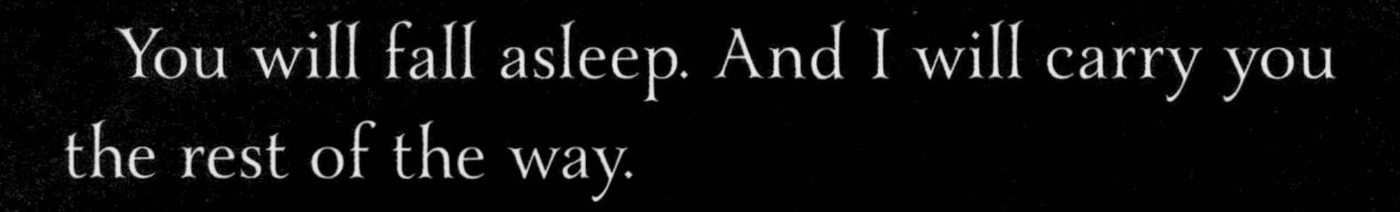

You will fall asleep. And I will carry you the rest of the way.

When you were born, you gave me my best job yet.